P9-CAB-849

Fly Paper

Tracy Kompelien

Illustrated by Anne Haberstroh

Consulting Editor, Diane Craig, M.A./Reading Specialist

ABDO
Publishing Company

Published by ABDO Publishing Company, 4940 Viking Drive, Edina, Minnesota 55435.

Copyright © 2007 by Abdo Consulting Group, Inc. International copyrights reserved in all countries. No part of this book may be reproduced in any form without written permission from the publisher. SandCastle™ is a trademark and logo of ABDO Publishing Company.

Printed in the United States.

Credits
Edited by: Pam Price
Curriculum Coordinator: Nancy Tuminelly
Cover and Interior Design and Production: Mighty Media
Photo Credits: ShutterStock

Library of Congress Cataloging-in-Publication Data

Kompelien, Tracy, 1975-
    Fly paper / Tracy Kompelien; illustrated by Anne Haberstroh.
        p. cm. -- (Fact & fiction. Critter chronicles)
    Summary: Freaky Fly, the food critic for the Flying Times, spies an error in his front-page review, but when he follows up, he finds an even tastier story. Alternating pages provide facts about houseflies.
    ISBN 10 1-59928-438-3 (hardcover)
    ISBN 10 1-59928-439-1 (paperback)

    ISBN 13 978-1-59928-438-5 (hardcover)
    ISBN 13 978-1-59928-439-2 (paperback)
    [1. Newspaper publishing--Fiction. 2. Food habits--Fiction. 3. Housefly--Fiction. 4. Flies--Fiction.]
I. Haberstroh, Anne, ill. II. Title. III. Series.

    PZ7.K83497Fly 2006
    [E]--dc22
                                                                                    2006005543

SandCastle Level: Fluent

SandCastle™ books are created by a professional team of educators, reading specialists, and content developers around five essential components—phonemic awareness, phonics, vocabulary, text comprehension, and fluency—to assist young readers as they develop reading skills and strategies and increase their general knowledge. All books are written, reviewed, and leveled for guided reading, early reading intervention, and Accelerated Reader® programs for use in shared, guided, and independent reading and writing activities to support a balanced approach to literacy instruction. The SandCastle™ series has four levels that correspond to early literacy development. The levels help teachers and parents select appropriate books for young readers.

| **Emerging Readers** | **Beginning Readers** | **Transitional Readers** | **Fluent Readers** |
| (no flags) | (1 flag) | (2 flags) | (3 flags) |

These levels are meant only as a guide. All levels are subject to change.

FACT & FICTION

This series provides early fluent readers the opportunity to develop reading comprehension strategies and increase fluency. These books are appropriate for guided, shared, and independent reading.

FACT The left-hand pages incorporate realistic photographs to enhance readers' understanding of informational text.

FICTION The right-hand pages engage readers with an entertaining, narrative story that is supported by whimsical illustrations.

The Fact and Fiction pages can be read separately to improve comprehension through questioning, predicting, making inferences, and summarizing. They can also be read side-by-side, in spreads, which encourages students to explore and examine different writing styles.

FACT OR FICTION? This fun quiz helps reinforce students' understanding of what is real and not real.

SPEED READ The text-only version of each section includes word-count rulers for fluency practice and assessment.

GLOSSARY Higher-level vocabulary and concepts are defined in the glossary.

SandCastle™ would like to hear from you.

Tell us your stories about reading this book. What was your favorite page? Was there something hard that you needed help with? Share the ups and downs of learning to read. To get posted on the ABDO Publishing Company Web site, send us an e-mail at:

sandcastle@abdopublishing.com

Flies soak food up with their spongelike
mouthparts.

Freaky Fly is the food critic
for *The Flying Times* newspaper.
He makes a living by flying
around town and reporting on
the best food in Antennaville.

Flies have compound eyes with up to 4,000 lenses in each eye. Their vision is blurry, but they are able to detect even the slightest motion.

Freaky, being a
very picky fly, wants to
check his column. He snatches
the first paper off the press. Suddenly
he yells, "Stop the presses!" All the
printing machines screech to a halt.

While most insects have four wings, flies
have only two. But flies are very skilled
fliers. They can hover, land on a ceiling,
and even fly backward!

Freaky's editor, Flashy, flies over to him and asks, "What is all this commotion about?"

"There is a big mistake on the map that accompanies my column!" Freaky exclaims.

Different flies eat the liquid from different things, including rotting meat and fruit, manure, nectar, blood, other insects, and most sweets.

Flies fly at an average speed of four and one-half miles per hour.

"If the map is wrong," Freaky says, "all the flies in Antennaville will go hungry tonight!"

But perhaps
the mistake isn't as bad
as it appears. Freaky decides he will
follow the map and see where it leads
him. He grabs the map and takes off.

Flies smell, taste, and feel with the hairs on their legs and bodies.

Unfortunately, Freaky becomes more disappointed as he follows the map. "There's not much cooking here. But what is that delicious scent?" he wonders as he rubs his legs together.

MR. DONUT

Flies taste with their feet. A fly's feet are
10 million times more sensitive than a
human tongue.

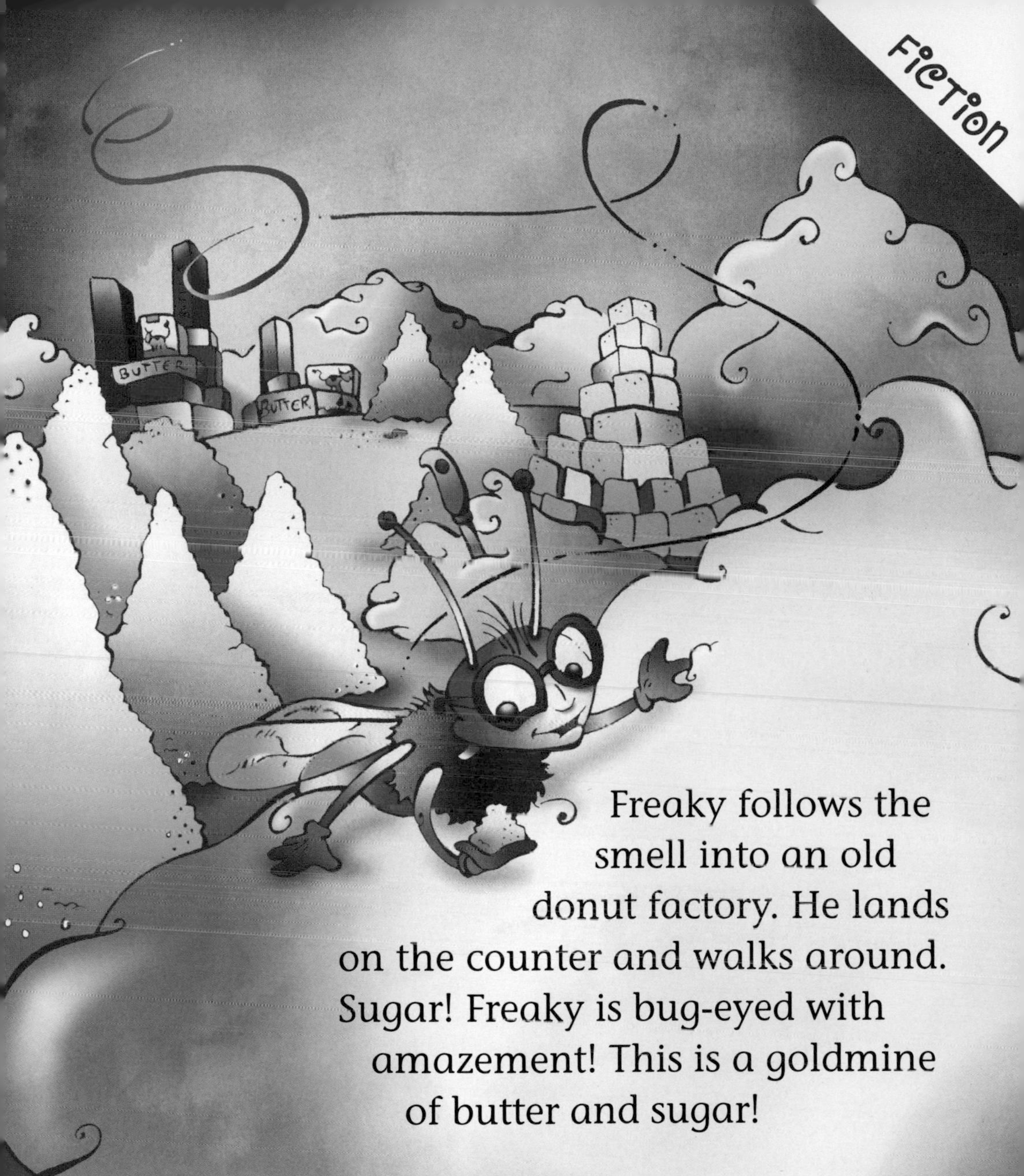

Freaky follows the
smell into an old
donut factory. He lands
on the counter and walks around.
Sugar! Freaky is bug-eyed with
amazement! This is a goldmine
of butter and sugar!

Flies are active during the day. They sleep during the night.

Freaky calls Flashy. "Start the presses! This mistake is the best one we've ever made!" The pressroom roars with delight as they make their deadline. The town of Antennaville goes to bed that night happy and full of butter and sugar.

FACT or Fiction?

Read each statement below. Then decide whether it's from the FACT section or the Fiction section!

1. Flies are food critics.

2. Flies can fly backward.

3. Flies taste with the hairs on their legs and bodies.

4. Flies use telephones to call each other.

ANSWERS
1. fiction 2. fact 3. fact 4. fiction

Flies soak food up with their spongelike mouthparts. 8

Flies have compound eyes with up to 4,000 lenses 17
in each eye. Their vision is blurry, but they are able to 29
detect even the slightest motion. 34

While most insects have four wings, flies have only 43
two. But flies are very skilled fliers. They can hover, 53
land on a ceiling, and even fly backward! 61

Different flies eat the liquid from different things, 69
including rotting meat and fruit, manure, nectar, 76
blood, other insects, and most sweets. 82

Flies fly at an average speed of four and one-half 93
miles per hour. 96

Flies smell, taste, and feel with the hairs on their 106
legs and bodies. 109

Flies taste with their feet. A fly's feet are 10 million 120
times more sensitive than a human tongue. 127

Flies are active during the day. They sleep during 136
the night. 138

Freaky Fly is the food critic for *The Flying Times* 10
newspaper. He makes a living by flying around 18
town and reporting on the best food in 26
Antennaville. 27

Freaky, being a very picky fly, wants to check 36
his column. He snatches the first paper off the 45
press. Suddenly he yells, "Stop the presses!" All 53
the printing machines screech to a halt. 60

Freaky's editor, Flashy, flies over to him and 68
asks, "What is all this commotion about?" 75

"There is a big mistake on the map that 84
accompanies my column!" Freaky exclaims. 89

"If the map is wrong," Freaky says, "all the flies 99
in Antennaville will go hungry tonight!" 105

But perhaps the mistake isn't as bad as it 114
appears. Freaky decides he will follow the map 122
and see where it leads him. He grabs the map 132
and takes off. 135

Unfortunately, Freaky becomes more disappointed as he follows the map. "There's not much cooking here. But what is that delicious scent?" he wonders as he rubs his legs together.

Freaky follows the smell into an old donut factory. He lands on the counter and walks around. Sugar! Freaky is bug-eyed with amazement! This is a goldmine of butter and sugar!

Freaky calls Flashy. "Start the presses! This mistake is the best one we've ever made!" The pressroom roars with delight as they make their deadline. The town of Antennaville goes to bed that night happy and full of butter and sugar.

GLOSSARY

blurry. lacking a definite outline

commotion. an excited disturbance

critic. one who makes a living by evaluating something such as food, theater, dance, or music

deadline. the time by which something must be completed

mistake. an error caused by lack of knowledge, poor judgement, or carelessness

newspaper. a paper containing current news that is usually printed and distributed daily or weekly

press. a machine that is used for printing

rot. to decay or decompose

vision. the ability to see

To see a complete list of SandCastle™ books and other nonfiction titles from ABDO Publishing Company, visit **www.abdopublishing.com** or contact us at: 4940 Viking Drive, Edina, Minnesota 55435 • 1-800-800-1312 • fax: 1-952-831-1632